SOMEBODY

SOMEBODY

Nancy Springer

Holiday House / New York

Library of Congress Cataloging-in-Publication Data

Springer, Nancy
Somebody / Nancy Springer.—1st ed.
p. cm
Summary: At the age of fifteen, a girl who has spent most of
her life moving around the country with her father and brother,
filling the emptiness inside her with chocolate, remembers her
real name, Sherica, and searches the Internet to learn the truth
about her mother and her own past.
ISBN 978–0–8234–2099–5 (hardcover)
[1. Parental kidnapping—Fiction.   2. Self-esteem—Fiction.
3. Identity—Fiction.   4. Fathers and daughters—Fiction.   5. Brothers
and sisters—Fiction.   6. Overweight persons—Fiction.   7. Names,
Personal—Fiction.   8. Moving, Household—Fiction.]   I. Title.
PZ7.S76846So 2009
[Fic]–dc22
2008020859

To my mother

SOMEBODY

1

AT THE TIME MY NAME was even more fattening than usual. I don't want to offend anybody who happens to have the same name, so I'll present this as a multiple-choice question: Of the following names, which is the one most likely to make a nothing-special teenage girl eat glazed jelly donuts until she practically turns into one?

a) *Debbie*

b) *Suzy*

c) *Louanne*

d) *Rose*

e) *Patty*

f) *Marsha*

g) *June*

h) *Nancy*

i)   *Ginny*

j)   *Dot*

The answer is all of the above, which I know because each of them had been my name, although not in that order, at one time or another since I was five.

It's funny how, whatever way you're raised, as a little kid you just figure it's okay and don't ask questions. I guess I was maybe twelve or thirteen when I started to realize it wasn't normal to change names as often as most families changed the calendar on their fridge. It wasn't normal to have a father and no mother, not even a weekend mother, either; and it wasn't normal, although it *was* kind of interesting, that my father's hobby was faking identification papers so that we could be new people each time we moved, which was once or twice a year, which, again, wasn't normal.

Now I was fifteen, give or take a year because my birthday kept getting switched around—which was *way* not normal—and I was thinking about these things a lot.

Especially since this latest move, which was just, like, last week. I'd been hoping, stupid me, that since Daddy had a girlfriend he really seemed to like in the town where we'd been, we might actually stay there for a while. But no such luck, I guess they had a fight, or something else bothered Daddy. He never says why, just tells us to pack. So off we went again. He had the documentation all ready, giving me the really fattening new name. See, Daddy, who is kind of a control freak, even if he is really nice about it, always insisted on "brainstorming" the new names himself as he "created" the documentation for our next move. The move itself was usually over Christmas or during the summer so that we'd start at a new school with our new names after a vacation break.

This time it was July. Daddy was Benjamin Caldwell, with shiny new business cards already printed up; my big brother, who is kind of a Daddy-clone, was Thomas Caldwell; and I was . . . never-mind-it-doesn't-matter Caldwell, shoving cold leftover four-cheese pizza into my face for breakfast.

As I reached for my third slice, Daddy said with that sunny smile of his, "That's my girl. Eat up, and pretty soon you're gonna be as big as your mother, with her blubber butt slopping over the sides of the Harley when she took off with that Italian guy."

My dad could say things like this and make it practically sound like a compliment. Daddy had that kind of personality. Good-looking, friendly, kind of down-home. He was a born salesman and never had any trouble finding a well-paying job, wherever we moved. Or any trouble keeping it because he could get away with just about anything if he smiled right. I mean, there he was at breakfast comparing me to my slut of a mother, and it almost felt okay.

Almost.

After I took a bite of pizza, I smiled back at Daddy the same way and said, "I don't remember Mom being all that fat."

Summer gives a person too much time to think. I'd been thinking, and I'd decided that the next time Daddy mentioned Mom—he never talked about her except to joke about her fooling around with men or running out on him—that there were other things I wanted to find out. Like her name, for gosh sake.

But before Daddy could answer, or even react, my brother yelled at me, with his mouth full of so-called muscle-building cereal, "What do *you* know? You were just a little kid!"

Yeah, like he was so much older, like, two years? "I wasn't talking to you," I said, keeping my eyes on Dad as I tried again. "Dad, the Italian guy with the motorcycle, was he the same one as the guy who had a ponytail?"

But at the same time, my brother asked, "Hey, Dad, where was Mom from?"

Dad grinned. "Oklahoma."

"Where in Oklahoma?"

"Tulsa."

And they both started laughing like gooney birds. See, Tulsa spelled backward is "a slut." It was one of their asinine jokes. Ha-ha-ha. Dad and my brother were buddies, thick like a bucket of ticks. It made me crazy.

I turned on my brother. "Why do you always do that?"

"Do what?" He was still snickering.

"Run interference when I try to talk to Dad."

No more snickering. "Well, you shouldn't be asking him questions!"

"Why not?"

"Do you think he *wants* to talk about that stuff?"

They had stopped laughing and were both looking at me in this superior sort of way, like special forces, like they'd served in Iraq together. Here I was trying to talk with Daddy, arguing with my stupid brother instead, getting so pissed that I opened my big mouth and out came something I never should have said.

"Why not? You think he's done something wrong?"

For the heaviest minute there was this silence like all the silence in my life had got compressed into a . . . I don't know . . . a black hole, a nuclear implosion. Instead of pizza, I felt like I'd swallowed a suicide bomb.

Then Dad brought his hand down on the table with a bang that made me jump an inch off the chair. "Now listen, both of you," he said not loudly, but for once there was no trace of a smile on his face. "It's not like I'm a criminal. I never murdered anybody or raped anybody. I never pulled a gun on anybody. I've never even hit anybody. Have I ever hit either of you?" His stare shot back and forth between my brother and me, not angry exactly but real intense. "Have I ever touched either of you the wrong way? Haven't I always made sure you each had your own bed in your own room? I work hard, I don't do crack or meth or anything like that, I don't drink, I don't even smoke; and neither of you has ever missed a meal. Isn't that so?"

"Yes, Daddy," I said.

"Yes, Dad," my brother said at the same time.

"Now I got to get to work." Leaving his unfinished coffee, Dad stood up, which meant the discussion—if you can call it that—was over, and he put his smile back in position on his face. He didn't need any tooth whitener, not my father, handsome and almost as much of a hunk as my athletic brother. Neither of them had any weight problem, not even a pot belly.

Dad beamed down at me. "Are you going to start up with the babysitting today, Blondie?" That was his current nickname for me, and it's not even like I'm naturally blond. I think my real hair color is kind of brown, because I get dark roots, but it's hard to say. At different times Dad had dyed it various shades of brown or red or black or blond until I got old enough to take over the job for myself.

My brother was required to dye his hair, too, pretty much the same color as the rest of us, whatever it might be at the time. But he didn't seem to mind our weird way of life. Whenever we moved to a new place, my brother would join a team, it didn't matter what sport, and then he'd have something to do and some new, instant friends. He was old enough to have a real part-time job but he never did. He just mowed a few lawns now and then.

"Sure, Daddy," I said, being a good girl again. "That's what I'll do, start to line up some babysitting."

2

Fifteen-year-old girl will babysit
Responsible, reliable, dependable

Fat, ugly, and nothing else to do, I thought as I hand-lettered the words on a plain sheet of paper. We always had plenty of paper around—for Daddy's hobby.

Available days, evenings, weekends

No life. I mean, maybe it would have been okay to be nobody—no talent, nothing special about me—if I was part of a group. But that wasn't going to happen, the way we were always moving and the way Daddy wouldn't let us bring other kids home. He didn't want anybody snooping around the house. Brian could go hang out with his sports buddies as much as he wanted, but I didn't have, like, a Nobody Club to join. I was never going to have any real friends or—or anybody. Unless . . . something . . . changed. . . .

That was as far as I could get consciously. Just far enough to know that something was wrong, something major was missing in my life; but I couldn't say exactly what. Stuff like this doesn't happen inside a person all at once. I'd been working up to it for months.

Maybe years. Trying to figure out this creepy feeling that I was being had. Noticing things. Like, the last time Daddy had joked about Mom running off with the guy on the motorcycle, it had been a Honda, not a Harley. And it had been the hippie guy with the gray ponytail, not some Italian guy.

All Daddy's stories about Mom—she was going around with a father and a son at the same time; she went skinny-dipping with a guy she met in a karaoke bar; she ran up a huge bill calling a phone sex line—sometimes it was a thousand dollars and other times, two thousand—they all kept changing a little. Sometimes a karaoke bar, some-times a biker bar, sometimes a truck stop.

When I was younger, I used to get all hot in my heart hearing Daddy talk about stuff like that, full of pity for my father, hating Mom for the things she'd done to him. Back then Dad was my capital-D Daddy, and Mom was the wicked witch. So it felt really weird now to be thinking about things in a different way, to say to myself, hey, if *I* was a married man watching my wife ride away with some guy on a motorcycle, I'd remember exactly who he was.

It felt worse than weird. It felt kind of sickening to realize that my dad's stories were just that. Stories.

Not to call them lies, exactly, but . . .

No. I couldn't think about it anymore.

Hollow feeling inside me.

Needed chocolate. Lots of chocolate.

I finished my flyer in a hurry by putting my most recent phone number a whole bunch of times across the bottom, then headed kazoomba downstairs to the kitchen. *Kazoomba* was the way I moved, according to my brother and Daddy. They said when I really got going, the fat went kazoomba to keep up with my arm and leg bones. But even though Daddy teased me about being fat, he always stocked plenty of my favorite goodies in the cupboard. As for the kazoomba, I wore extra-large T-shirts to hide it, with big screen prints across the front because I didn't wear a bra. It would have been too embarrassing—I mean, to ask Dad to take me shopping for that kind of thing—and then go around with my front sticking out. I just couldn't. It was better to be fat all over.

Slamming open one kitchen cupboard door after another—damn—being in a new place again, not knowing where anything was—finally I found—excellent!—a big bag of cookies, not just chocolate chip but chocolate *chunk*. Sticking two of them into my mouth at once, I carried the bag with me as I headed out the door.

You'd think that, with all the places I'd lived all over the country, they'd seem different from each other; but somehow they all seemed the same. Dad always found us the same sort of rental house, run-down but okay, in a cracked-sidewalk neighborhood in the same sort of place, too big for a town but not quite a real city; no museums or colleges or anything like that, but always a Wal-Mart and a McDonald's and a Taco Bell. And a shopping mall. And all those places would be out along some highway, too far away for me to walk to.

But heading out of my new "home"—ha!—in my flip-flops to show off my turquoise toenails and give people something that wasn't going kazoomba to look at, I mentally predicted what I'd find within walking distance of the rental house: a gas station with junk food and lottery tickets, a YMCA for my muscle-head brother, a hair-and-nail salon, a coin laundry, a beverage distributor, a check casher, a karate studio, a tattoo shop, a notary public, a drugstore maybe with a photocopy machine . . . that was what I was looking for first, a photocopier so I could run off flyers to put up in the coin laundry, et cetera.

I found it in a shop in a corner storefront. The sign said HANDY HARDWARE AND LOCKSMITH, but in the window display space sat a photocopier. When I went in I saw tools and stuff on one side but ceramics on the other. Instead of just smelling like WD-40 oil and rubber and metal, it also smelled like gift wrap and Magic Marker and paint, but not house paint—craft paint. Behind the counter sat an older woman painting a ceramic hedgehog. I guessed maybe her husband was the locksmith.

I like funky little stores like that, all mixed up. Right away I liked the middle-aged woman minding the place because she gave me a for-real smile, not just a display of teeth, and because anybody could tell she was really good at what she was doing, the way she handled her little paintbrush, and because she looked like she could handle life or whatever, no problem.

"How can I help you, honey?" she asked, with the hedgehog, really cute, in one hand and her paintbrush in the other. It was a tiny brush. She was working on the eyes.

I explained that I needed to make some photocopies. She said to help myself, they were ten cents apiece or if I made twenty or more the price went down to seven cents apiece. I made twenty, and while I was running them, I told her I liked her nails, which were manicured to match her lipstick but not too long. She said thank you, she had them done at Lucy's, and wasn't it a nice day for July, not too humid. Stuff like that. But then, just as I gathered up my copies to go pay for them, I blurted out, "What I need is a place where I can buy some time on a computer the way you buy time on a photocopier."

"You need what, hon?" She set the half-painted hedgehog aside.

"Um, a computer." Dad kept his door padlocked. He wouldn't let my brother or me near the computer in his bedroom, and he wouldn't buy us one of our own, either. He said we couldn't afford it, but I think he didn't want us getting on the Internet. Like I mentioned, he was kind of a control freak about some things, such as no cameras or camera phones—or any kind of cell phones, for that matter—and no family photos, and in general lots of Daddy rules that had been okay with me until lately, when I had started to ask questions—at least to myself.

And what had got me started asking questions was the stupid bra situation, of all things. No, that's not true. It was before that, a couple of years ago when I got my first period, and I didn't even know what it was. It happened in the middle of world-history class, and really freaked me out. I could feel a wetness, like I was ruptured or something, but I couldn't see it. I asked to go to the bathroom, and when I got there and saw blood all over my pants, I thought I was going to die. I mean, I'd heard about menstruation in health class, but who ever pays attention to anything they tell you in health class? Anyhow, I didn't know it was going to be like *this*. I ran bawling to the school nurse and after she'd fixed me up and tried to calm me down, she wanted to call my mother. Oh, I didn't have a mother? What had happened to her? So I told her Mom ran off, but somehow in that mess it was like I woke up and had this feeling that it wasn't true.

And then later that evening, at Wal-Mart, when I was standing in front of the totally confusing shelves of "feminine hygiene products," all embarrassed from asking my Dad to drive me there, I didn't know whether to get pads or tampons and what kind or size or anything, and I didn't have anybody to ask.

And that wasn't right.

Well, I got through it okay on my own, of course, but I guess that was the day I started wanting some answers— not that I've been able to get any out of Daddy yet, or my brother, either. You would think that being older, my brother would remember things, and maybe he did, but he wouldn't talk. He was so all about Daddy, it was like they were a two-person secret society, my very own mini-Mafia. I kept trying, like this morning, but it was no use. So now here I was asking about computers.

Ringing up my bill, the Handy Hardware woman asked, "Don't they have computers in the schools these days?"

"Yeah, but . . ." I'd already thought about the school computers, how there was never enough time, always somebody else waiting for a turn, and a teacher or, even worse, my brother, looking over my shoulder.

"But it's summer. The schools aren't *open*. Silly me."

The woman charged me $1.40 plus tax, then said, "I think they have computers in the public library, too."

I'd never been in a public library in my life. "They do?"

"I think so. You could go see, honey. It's right around the corner."

Oh. Oh my gosh, the town library was supposed to be far away like the Red Lobster. Things were going too fast. "I, um, I have to put these flyers up first."

"Would you like to borrow a pair of scissors?"

"Huh? Oh." Duh, I needed to cut a fringe of phone-number tabs at the bottom of each flyer. "No, that's okay. I'll, um, I'll do them at home." I liked her, yet I felt in a hurry to get away from her, as if I'd already let her find out too much about me. Daddy would freak if he knew. "Thank you." I headed toward the door.

"You forgot your bag of cookies," she called.

"Oh. Um, thanks, but you eat them; I don't want them." Which goes to show how badly I needed to get out of there.

I went straight home, if you can call a place where we'd lived for less than a week "home." Bare, like all the other places, because we never accumulated much. No place mats or anything pretty on the kitchen table where I was sitting, cutting the tabs on my flyers when my brother walked in.

Right away he started in on me. "Listen up, Blob. I

want to talk to you. Are you crazy, asking Dad questions? Are you stupid?"

I felt so tired from the gymnastics going on inside my head, that I didn't say anything. I just sat there.

Which turned out to be a good thing because he kept blabbing. "Are you really that dumb? Haven't you figured it out?"

This time what kept me from saying anything was that I felt a sudden strong urge to jab him with the scissors, or at least throw them at him. It took all my concentration to let go of them and lay them on the table.

When I didn't reply, he gave a kind of horse snort and said, "You really don't have a clue, do you?" and he sat down on the opposite side of the table, sighed, and started acting more like a big brother, like he ought to take care of me. "Listen," he said, keeping his voice very low like there might be neighbors eavesdropping at the screen door, "isn't it pretty obvious that Dad's on the run from something?"

I just nodded, listening hard because none of us had ever said this before. It fell in the same category as what I'd said that morning: Something we never talked about. But lately I'd begun to suspect why my father was running, or from what, and it really freaked me out. It spooked me so bad that I denied everything, like Daddy did.

"But really, he's not a criminal," I said.

"Not in his own mind." I couldn't remember when I'd last heard my brother's voice so thoughtful, almost gentle. "When Dad said that, he meant he never murdered anybody, or—"

"I heard what he said." I kept my voice low, too, and shut up quick because I was totally scared of the things I wanted to say.

My brother said quietly, "I think what he *did* do was, like, steal money or something. Maybe from somebody he worked for. Maybe he forged checks, or did some fancy math."

Huh. I wondered whether Dad had told him that, it was so, like, *nothing* compared to what I was thinking.

"You know how tricky Dad can be," my brother said.

"Sure."

"He's really kind of a con artist," my brother bragged. "He's good."

Yeah, Dad was good all right. Too good. Hadn't my brother ever thought that Dad might be conning us too? But I couldn't say it. I just nodded.

"He'll get away with it forever if we don't mess up. So *stop it with the stupid questions*. Trying to make trouble." Just like that my brother quit acting human and reverted to being a jerk. He stood up and leaned over me until his face was just a few inches from mine. Whispering between his teeth he demanded, "Don't you know one thing leads to another? Do you want our father to go to jail?"

The idea of Dad in jail scared me so much that my brother's stupid gorilla act scared me too. "Let me alone! I'll tell Daddy." I sounded about six years old.

"Oh, for crying out loud," my brother muttered as he turned away and headed out the door.

3

I DON'T REMEMBER HOW MANY days it took me. Three, four, five, maybe even a week. Posting my babysitting flyers in the coin laundry and the Kwik-Stop Mini Mart and all those other places, I walked past the public library half a dozen times, but I could only manage to look at it for a few seconds each time, even though it was just an ugly concrete-block building.

"It used to be a neighborhood bowling alley, six lanes," the woman at Handy Hardware and Locksmith explained next time I dropped in. "I like your earrings, dear."

"Thank you." They were big bright plastic daisies. I had an even bigger pair, yellow butterflies, and—well, never mind the green frog earrings. What I'm trying to say is it helped me feel happier, sort of, to wear that kind of stuff, the funkier the better. I liked hair clips with ribbons, and little flower stickers to put on my fingernails, and things some people would call tacky, like hand-painted ceramic hedgehogs.

Today the woman at the hardware store was painting a ceramic searchlight and taking care of customers while I taped my flyer in one corner of her front window. "Has anybody called you about babysitting yet, sweetie?"

"Just one. Last night."

"Well, you'll have more when word gets around."

Yeah, and when I got busy babysitting I wouldn't have much time for . . .

Couldn't think about it.

Had to.

For going to the library and getting on the computer and looking for answers.

Just thinking it, I needed a chocolate fix, quick. "Do you still have those cookies?" I asked Adelle—that was the lady's name. I'd been stopping by to talk about nail polish and stuff and watch her paint, and she'd told me to call her Adelle.

She had a real name.

So did I.

Except I wasn't supposed to say it, ever, or think about it. I was supposed to forget about it, and my father and brother probably thought I had. They didn't think I had much brain inside my blubber.

But I did. Even when I was a little kid five years old, I already knew how to spell my name and how to write it.

My whole name. The only name I've ever had that was not fattening. Of course I remembered it.

The name I—

I knew what I needed to do.

But I didn't know whether it would help. Or whether it might make things worse. A lot worse.

"Absolutely, I still have them, right here," said Adelle, setting down the searchlight she was painting—lighthouse, I mean. I get those two words mixed up, *searchlight* and *lighthouse*. Like to me they're both looking for something lost: *searchlight* looking for a lost airplane in the dark sky, and *lighthouse* looking for a lost ship at sea. That may not be even close to what they really do, but that's the way I imagine them.

Adelle ducked under the counter and came up holding the bag of chocolate chunk cookies. "Here you go, honey."

I grabbed for the cookie bag like I was drowning and it was a life preserver. I jammed cookies into my mouth, one, two, *three,* all at once.

Adelle didn't say a word, but she did kind of stare at me. I looked down at my blubber, hating myself.

Hating me. And that's when I thought, how much worse could things get?

I managed to swallow what I had in my mouth.

"Have some more," Adelle invited. "Take them with you."

"No, thank you," I whispered, shoving the bag of cookies into her hands, then backing away like she was pointing a gun at me. "I gotta go do something."

And I did. I had to do it *now*. Now, before I chickened out.

I wonder whether anybody had ever walked into that little town library trembling before. I doubt it. There were only maybe half a dozen people in there, browsing the shelves or sitting around with newspapers; but I didn't appreciate it that every single one of them looked at me. Of course all they would notice was the kazoomba aspect of me, not that I was scared. I'd known for a long time that fat was good for something: It was good to hide behind.

Inside, the town library looked pretty much like a school library, except not so bright. Dark old pictures on the walls instead of posters. Chairs and tables and checkout counter were kind of dark wood, too. Smelled like wax. Behind the counter a boy was reading something, a teenage boy who showed every sign of being a real loser, socially I mean. A book nerd. Khaki pants belted under his armpits, striped short-sleeved button-front shirt that looked like it had come from the Goodwill. Haircut that looked like his mother did it at home. Skinny like a lizard, narrow-shouldered, pimply, and I'm not saying any of this to put him down because who am I to diss anybody? I appreciated that he was the only person in the place not staring at me. Didn't even look up from his reading until I stood in front of him. Then his brown eyes blinked as if he'd been sleeping and I'd woken him up.

The only way I could control my shaky voice was by whispering. "Is there a computer I can use to get on the Internet?"

"Sure. Do you have your library card?"

"Um, no, I . . . didn't know I needed one."

"Do you live here?" He might have been a loser, but his voice was a winner—like it should have come from a guy who looked like a movie star, or from a movie star playing the role of a really nice, strong, and comforting hero. He took the name and address I gave him, gave me a library card, and then instead of just pointing me toward the computer, he came out from behind the desk, led me to the far side of the room, and turned it on for me.

"All right?"

I barely heard him, sitting in front of the computer like I'd never seen one before. It seemed awfully bright, like a searchlight. I kept blinking. He asked, "Is there anything else I can help you with?"

I whispered, "How do I look for, um . . ." Just in time I stopped myself.

He didn't even ask what. Wasn't nosy. "You want to Google something?" He showed me how. "If it's more than one word, put quote marks around them," he advised before he went away.

It was more than one word. I put quote marks around them. I felt my fingers fumbling as I typed them into the Google box on the computer screen. I felt my hand faltering on the mouse, struggling to get the pointer where I needed it.

There. I clicked.

SEARCH.

I felt like I couldn't breathe.

But then, in the paper-rustling quiet of the public library, out of me came a sound I didn't intend and can barely describe. Maybe a little bit like a baby's first cry.

I noticed heads turned to stare at me, but I didn't care.

Because from the lit-up computer screen a really cute little girl was smiling at me, and she *was* me. Sort of. I didn't recognize myself so much as I remembered the picture, my kindergarten photo, and I knew the *dress*. I had loved that sky-blue dress with yellow-bead trim around the neck. Mommy had made yellow beaded barrettes to go with it; there they were in my strawberry-blonde hair.

Mommy.

HELP THIS GIRL'S DESPERATE MOTHER FIND HER, begged the heading over my picture.

Mom—she *did* care! She did want me.

But—maybe not. The first photo was like a hug, but the next one was like a slap in the face, "age enhanced," the text explained, "to show the missing girl as she might appear now."

Gorgeous.

Slim, smiling, happy, healthy, loved. And so beautiful. So not me.

But it was *supposed* to be me.

Oh, God.

I couldn't stand it. I couldn't think. I couldn't get up and go away. I couldn't take my eyes off the screen. I saw words and words and other pictures, yet I couldn't comprehend them. I don't know how long I sat there staring, like the glare of the computer had made me blind.

Deaf, too. I gradually became aware that someone was talking to me. The geeky boy from the desk, standing beside me and telling me in his velvet voice that somebody else wanted to get on the computer now. Using that stupid, fattening name I'd told him to put on my library card.

I turned and looked at him. Then, out of a place way deep inside me, I said, "Sherica," and my voice sounded quiet and sure.

"I beg your pardon?"

"Sherica. Rhymes with America. Suloff."

"Excuse me?"

"My name is Sherica Suloff." I might have sounded calm, but I'm sure I didn't look it. I guess I stood up, but I don't remember blundering out the door.

4

I don't remember walking back to the rental house, either. The next thing I remember is standing at the door of my brother's bedroom, which had sheets over the windows for curtains instead of on the bed—he slept on the bare mattress. Right now he was lying on it, but not exactly loafing. He was squeezing a biceps-building gizmo in each hand. He had his music on but not too loud—the neighbors had complained already. He'd heard me come thumping up the stairs and was giving me a look, like, what's the matter with you?

"Brian," I said, not even loud.

"What?" Both squeeze-grips sprang out of his hands. At the same time as they hit the floor, so did my brother's feet. He shot off the bed and killed his CD with one whack. "Are you crazy? Don't call me that!"

"From now on I'm going to call you by your real name.

Bri, Dad stole something all right, but it wasn't money. It was us."

He took a step toward me. "Are you out of your *mind*?"

Even to me I sounded kind of loony tunes. "He robbed us." I meant that two ways: He had taken *us* away from Mom, and he had taken something important *from* us.

"What the hell are you talking about?" Standing almost a foot taller than I was, fists clenched, arms spraddled like he was carrying a watermelon under each one, Bri didn't look a thing like his age-enhanced picture—Jeez, I just then realized that his photo was on the Web site, too, along with a computer-generated image of a slim, smiling, handsome boy who didn't look a bit like the beefy bunghead glaring at me.

"We don't either of us look like we're supposed to," I said. "I wonder if Dad did that on purpose."

"Would you please make *sense*?"

I was making as much sense as I could when I felt like my mind was swimming and couldn't touch bottom. "Dad's picture was on the Web site, too."

"*What* Web site?" Each time he yelled he took another step toward me.

Up to my neck in a dream or a nightmare, not sure which, I said, "Mom's trying to find us."

Instantly, gut reaction, loud like a slammed door, "She is not!" Brain shouted.

"Monica Suloff." How in the world could I have forgotten Mom's name, when she'd put her mother's name, Sherry, together with her own name, Monica, to call me Sherica? "Your mom," I added. "My mom. Our mom. She's looking for us."

"No! She's a slut!"

I shook my head.

"Brian—"

"Don't call me that!"

I understand now how bad I was scaring him. I mean, he and Dad were as close as twins. All he wanted was Dad, and Dad was all he had.

But at the time I could barely figure out what was going on in me, much less in him. I said, "I have to. It's your name. Brian—"

He hit me.

Not with his fist. Open hand. He whacked me across the face, not even hard, more like he was trying to swat a bug. But I was already so shaky, he knocked me off-balance, and I fell.

Next thing I knew I was bawling so hard I couldn't see. I mean, it wasn't like he'd hurt me at all, but he'd never hit me before. I sobbed so hard I couldn't say any of the things I wanted to scream at him.

"Hey, are you okay? I'm sorry, I didn't mean to . . ." He pulled on my arms, trying to get me up off the floor. Then, when that didn't work, he ran out of the room, came back with a wet washcloth, kneeled down beside me, and poked at my eyes with it. I pushed him away, sat up, took the cloth, and wiped my face; I blew my nose on it, balled it up, and threw it at him.

He ducked. "I guess you're okay."

"Go to hell."

"Hey, I said I'm sorry. I didn't mean to get physical. You made me do it, saying crazy stuff."

"It's not crazy!" With my nose all clogged, it probably sounded like "idz dot gravy," but at least I was telling him. "Id's true. I saw id. Mom—"

"Okay, so Mom's on the Internet. So what?" His voice was rising again. "She's still a slut, and we don't want anything to do with her."

From downstairs came the sound of a door, and Dad calling, "Yo! Anybody home?"

"Oh, God!" Bri whispered. "Listen, you can't say anything to Dad! You can't!" Then he yelled, "Up here, Dad!"

"Well, supper's down here. This town has the best Chinese I've ever tasted." From what I'd heard, there weren't many dads like Dad who always came home from work in a good mood. "I brought takeout. Come on!"

"Coming!" Brian gave me a look that tried to be a warning but seemed more, like, panicked, as he ran downstairs.

"Blondie?" Dad called.

"Coming." I followed more slowly, all mixed up. About

Dad. Because of the things he'd done, in a way Daddy had whacked me a lot harder than Bri. But I couldn't help it. The minute I walked into the kitchen, the minute Dad looked at me with his special smile, I started to cry; and I ran to him and hugged him as hard as I could.

"Hey! What's the matter, little girl?" Little, ha. Only Daddy would call me little. He put his arms around me and patted my back, letting me cry on his shoulder. "What's wrong?"

"N-n-nothing."

"We were fighting," my brother said, sounding totally normal except his mouth wasn't full of wontons yet.

"About what?"

"Nothing."

"You kids." Dad didn't want to know what it was about, not really. My brother couldn't help being a boy, Dad usually said, and I was supposed to stay out of testosterone's way. He gave me a squeeze and said, "Settle down, baby girl. Hey, I brought home ice cream, too, how about that? Strawberry, your favorite. Would you like some right now?"

And there I was hating me again because yes, I would.

So I sat at the table, and Daddy brought me a big bowl of ice cream with Hershey's chocolate syrup on top. And I ate it. Then I ate another one. Then I ate fried rice and sesame chicken. Daddy said, "Eat up. There's more where that came from." I had stopped crying because it's impossible to bawl and chow down on egg rolls at the same time. And I kept stuffing my face because there was nothing else I could do. Because if I told anybody about me, who I really was, if Daddy got caught, they'd put him in jail.

And I just couldn't do that. Not to Daddy. No matter what.

My brother had gone out to meet his buddies down at the basketball court, but I was still eating. Daddy was sitting with me at the table when we heard a sound we're not used to.

Somebody knocking at the door.

I jumped. If Daddy jumped, too, he didn't show it, but I saw his eyebrows go up. Wherever we lived, we always kept to ourselves, and here we'd just moved in.

Knock, knock. Not hard. Polite.

"Just a minute," Daddy called, scraping his chair back from the table. He strode to the door and looked out the peephole. Then he opened the door.

I felt like somebody had punched me in the gut. There on our doorstep stood the skinny, dweeby boy from the library.

5

"Hi," SAID THE LIBRARY BOY to my father. "Sorry to bother you, but I'm going around asking everybody. Do you know who this dog belongs to?"

"No, I don't. He's a cute little fella!" Dad likes dogs, even though he won't let us have any pets because we move around so much. I saw Dad stoop down to say hello to the dog, although I couldn't see the dog itself from where I was sitting.

What I did see was the library boy looking into the house straight at me and kind of signaling me with his eyes. Those brown eyes of his could, like, speak. Nearly as clearly as his velvet voice.

"Where'd you find him?" Dad asked, still patting the dog.

I knew in my aching gut that this wasn't really about the dog, but the skinny boy from the library said earnestly,

"Out by the old chicken-feed factory. He's a she, actually, and if I can't find her owner, I'm going to have to take her to Animal Control."

I thought I could not take any more today, but forced myself to get up because I knew I wouldn't be able to sleep until I found out what the library boy wanted.

I knew it was me he'd come to find. I'd given him the address when I got my library card, and his showing up here was no coincidence.

Making myself walk over to the door, I could finally see the dog, a little mutt with a lot of long fur kind of the color and texture of overcooked spaghetti. That was the way it looked to me at the time. Normally I would have been cooing, "Ooooh, aren't you adorable," and patting it the way my Dad was.

"Do you know whose dog this is, Pattycake?" Dad asked me, playing a kind of game like we'd lived in that town for a while and knew some people.

I guess I surprised him when I answered, "Um, yeah, I think I saw it somewhere. . . ."

"Where?" asked the library boy promptly.

"I, um . . ." I flapped my hand around. "I don't know the name of the street. I could show you. It's not far."

"Really? That would be awesome!"

"Sure. No problem." I didn't give Daddy a chance to react, just said, "I'll be back in a little bit," and walked off with the brown-eyed boy and the little mutt tugging at the end of a length of rope.

I wanted this Sherlock to know I wasn't stupid, so when we got far enough away from the house, I asked, "What's your dog's name?"

He smiled. "Strudel."

"Do you normally walk her on a rope and go around—"

"No, she has a collar and leash for everyday purposes. My name is Mason, by the way."

"And you think you're a brain," I said.

He sighed around the edges of his smile. "I *know* I'm a brain, and I know I'm a nerd, and I try to be the best nerd I can be. Here we are."

He'd led me around a corner to a funky little park in between two streets that made a Y. It was just grass, three scrawny trees, petunias, a statue of a fireman, and a bench.

"Better have a seat, Sherica," Mason said.

Sherica. Something about the way he said my real name told me he didn't intend it as a threat, but it still went through me like a wild ride on a roller coaster, scary, but thrilling, too. I sat on the bench mostly because I felt weak in the knees.

Mason sat beside me, and without saying another word he reached into his shirt and pulled out a bunch of papers neatly stacked and stapled together, kind of like a school assignment. When he handed the papers to me, I just stared at the top one like I'd never seen it before.

But I had. Except, before, I'd seen it on a computer screen, in color. Not on paper in black and white.

"You left it open," Mason explained in that soft, musical voice of his, "and I printed it out before I closed it so the next person could go on-line. Then, later, when I got a chance, I looked you up on some other sites, like, The National Center for Missing & Exploited Children . . ."

Exploited described how I felt, although I couldn't explain why. All of a sudden I reached down and started patting Strudel. Good dog. Warm, felt like a dog, smelled like a dog, too. Solid, ordinary, real. Nice dog, there when I needed him.

". . . and printed them for you, too. It's all there, how your dad abducted . . ."

Abducted. My mind got stuck on that word, too, and I had to catch up with the rest of what Mason was saying.

". . . you and your brother, and how to contact your mother."

It was as if this library kid had prepared a report for me, but I didn't move to look at any of the other pages in it, and I didn't thank him. The thing felt like a snake in my hands, and I wanted to throw it back at him, yet my fingers clutched it. My voice had to fight its way out, all squeaky. "What are you going to do?"

"Do?" Mason looked at me with a quizzical smile. "I've already done it."

"You're not going to call the cops?"

"No."

"Or my mom?"

"No. But I wish I could."

"No, you don't. She doesn't want us," I explained, "my brother and me. She doesn't care about us. All she cares about is running around with her boyfriends." That was what Daddy had always said.

"If that's so, then how come she's going to so much trouble and expense to find you? It isn't easy to set up a Web site, you know."

"Shut up," I said. "Just shut up. You think I should call her. Why don't you call her?"

"I told you, I wish I could. I'd love to be a hero." Duh. Squeaky clean. He smelled like soap. "I'd have done it this afternoon a minute after you left the library if I could have."

"Well, why can't you?"

He just sat there, silent. Finally he stood up. "You'd better hide those papers so your father doesn't see them until you figure out what to do. Any way I can help, just let me know. Come on, Strudel." He and his dog walked off into the graying dusk.

6

I STASHED THE PAPERS UNDER my clothes, in the elastic waist of my shorts, hidden under my T-shirt, which was as big as a tent. When I got back to the house, I took the papers to my bedroom, put them out of sight, and left them there. I didn't look at them.

Not that day.

Or the next.

What to do? What did I *want*? I thought I knew what I wanted, which was to have, you know, a normal mom-dad-kids kind of family in a normal house with photographs of camping trips and reunions and stuff on the walls, and have some friends I fit in with, and stay in the same town for a few years.

What it looked like I could actually *have* was either Mom or Dad. Not both.

I knew Dad, and I didn't know Mom.

I loved Dad. I couldn't remember Mom well enough to know if I loved her.

But I didn't feel good about Dad.

I didn't feel good, period. There was this emptiness inside. I felt awful. So bad that even double-stuffed Oreos didn't help.

And the emptiness kept getting worse.

Until I just had to do something.

It must have been four or five days after Mason gave me the printouts that I finally marched up to my room and shut the door. Like just about every bedroom door in every rental house I'd lived in, this one didn't lock or even latch properly. But it didn't matter right now because there was nobody home except me. Which was a good thing because I had felt Brian watching me for further signs I was going "out of my mind."

Daddy, on the other hand, hadn't noticed anything, even though I was barely able to talk. To him, whenever I felt bad, it was just one of my "female" moods. Sure, he hugged me and called me his little girl and all that, but sometimes I thought he wouldn't really care if I never opened my big mouth except to shove chocolate into it.

Just in case Brian came home suddenly, I pushed a chair under the doorknob before I pulled the papers out of their hiding place under my mattress.

Trying to get myself started, I flipped through all the pages first. There were about seventeen phone numbers that anyone who spotted me was supposed to call, local and state and federal cop numbers and lawyer numbers and several associations' 800 numbers. Jeez, there were mug shots from what must have been every missing-person site on the Web, police reports—Mason must have followed every link he could find—newspaper articles—

A photograph of a woman caught my eye.

And it hit me like a tsunami, a huge wave drowning me, sweeping me away before my mind could form the word.

Mom.

One look at her, and I started sobbing. Tears poured down my face, soaking my shirt. It took me totally by surprise. Up till then I couldn't have told you what my mother looked like. I was sure I didn't remember, and I didn't think I'd recognize her if I met her on the street.

So it really shook me up, how every inch of me knew her all at once in some bone-deep way I can barely describe.

And loved her.

Yes, I loved my mom.

Or was it the little girl in me loving a mommy from ten years ago?

Seeing Mom's photo pretty much wiped me for that day. But the next day I got the papers out again.

Had to.

Once I'd finally started, I couldn't stop.

It must have taken me another four or five days to get through them. Now I took them one page at a time. Heck, sometimes one *line* at a time was all I could handle. For instance, I got stuck for hours on my missing persons report, my D.O.B. Date of birth. I had a birthday. I had an age. I figured it out: Fifteen years, five months, and three days. Then I had to just lie on my bed for a while, staring at the glow-in-the-dark stars I had stuck on the ceiling before I could go on to the next line: Place of birth: Latrobe, Pennsylvania. I was from someplace. I had a name, an age, and I was from Pennsylvania. For maybe an hour I'd have to sit and stare. It was like my mind couldn't handle so much normalcy.

Even once I got moving along I would reread pages or paragraphs over and over as if they were in a foreign language. ". . . last seen exiting Idlewild Park, Ligonier, Pennsylvania, with their father. . . ." Idlewild, beautiful name, and with it came memories more vague than a dream, of a wooden roller coaster, of carousel ponies with real horsehair tails. Last seen by what person? The girl at the petting zoo? The popcorn vendor? The ice-cream man?

Or Mom?

There I sat kind of in suspended animation, reaching

back with my mind, when *thump*, bang, *slam*, and here came Brian, charging into my room. He must have sneaked into the house to try to catch me by surprise. But the chair under the doorknob held him up just long enough. I had time to drop the printouts behind the bed and grab a magazine instead before he came barreling in, yelling, "What the hell are you hiding out in here for?"

"What are you busting in here for?" I yelled at the same time.

"You're up to something in here! What are you doing?"

"Didn't anybody ever teach you to *knock*? What if I was naked?"

"You'd better not be in the middle of the day. What you got there?" He grabbed the magazine out of my hands. It happened to be one that I had sneaked out of the stuff he kept hidden under *his* mattress. I ought to find a better hiding place for my papers; if Brian snooped in my room, under the mattress was the first place he'd look.

Especially now that he knew I'd found *his* secret. His face went as red as his pimples. "You shouldn't be looking at that!"

"Like you should?"

"You keep your fat hands off my stuff!"

"You stay out of my room!"

Et cetera. Just another fight. But I knew Brian was

scared, had been ever since that day I had called him by his real name, and I knew he wasn't going to let it go. He would be back.

"I need a chain or something, to keep people *out* of my bedroom when I'm *in* it," I explained to Adelle at the hardware store. She was painting a little pinto pony today, really cute. "No hurry," I added, even though she probably knew that, the way I liked to hang out and watch her paint. "Finish what you're doing."

"Thank you, sweetheart. I have to make sure I get the spots right. Horse spots look different than cow spots or dog spots, have you ever noticed?" She was making a tan shadow line around the edge of the pony's brown markings. "I'll be right with you. How's the babysitting coming, hon?"

"Good. And thanks again for letting me list you as a reference." I'd had several jobs. And instead of spending my money on manicures and pedicures and funky earrings the way I usually did, I was saving every cent of it, hiding it from Brian and Daddy, although I couldn't say why, not even to myself.

"I'm sure you're a very good babysitter. . . . There." She set the pony down and put her paintbrush into water she kept on the counter in a plastic cup; then she got up to help me. "We have chains," she said, "and bolts, but the simplest thing—do you need to install this yourself?"

"Yes."

"Well, the easiest would be a good old-fashioned hook."

She explained to me how to make a hole in the wood with something sharp to get the screw tips started, and then I should be able to twist the parts in by hand.

"It's none of my business, honey pie," she told me as I paid her, "but if something's wrong at home, you can come here, all right?"

I nodded and muttered, "Thank you. But it's not like that." And I thought, I *have* to find another place to hide those papers.

Adelle said, "Good. I'm glad to hear it. But if you ever do have any problems, I'd be happy to help."

And, surprise, my mouth opened and words popped out. "Do you know the skinny boy, Mason's his name, who works at the library?"

"Mason Kufta?" She smiled. "Yes, everybody knows the Kuftas. Decent, hardworking people."

I hadn't realized until I mentioned Mason how badly I needed somebody to talk with about all the weirdness going on in—not in my life, not yet, but in me—and Mason was the only one who knew what it was about. "Do you know where they live?"

"Why, over on Butternut Street." Adelle gave me a second look, and her smile faded. "You're not thinking of getting, ah, involved with Mason, are you, sweetie?"

I could have laughed out loud. "You mean like a boyfriend? That'll never happen."

"Why not?"

"Because I'm fat, that's why not."

"Fat?" Her eyebrows shot up. "What ever put that idea into your head? Why, honey, you don't weigh a bit more than I do, and you're taller. Do you look at me and think I'm fat?"

"No! Um, not at all." She was a little chunky, maybe, but she looked okay.

She was shaking her head. "Girls these days . . . you just need to get an underwire bra and some clothes that fit you, that's all, and be proud of what you've got, some meat on your bones, the way God meant a woman to look."

For some reason this embarrassed me way more than being called fat ever had, and anyway, what did she know? Fat for a teenager wasn't the same as fat for an old lady. I knew I was as fat as a hippo, but I didn't want to argue with her. "Um, where did you say Mason lived?" I asked to change the subject.

"Butternut Street. It's really just a lane, on the east edge of town . . . but please don't let yourself get too fond of Mason, sweetie."

"Why not? He's nice."

"Yes, the whole family is nice." Adelle took a deep breath and turned to stare out the window. "But just keep in mind, not every illegal alien comes from Mexico. Nothing against the Kuftas. And that's all I'm going to say."

7

THAT NIGHT I HAD A babysitting job, which usually means little kids but this time actually meant a baby. Like, an infant, only three months old; and it looked like he was his parent's first, and this was their first night out since he'd been born. The baby watched quietly from his rock-a-bye chair while they fussed. They acted like they were going on a cruise to Alaska, not just out for dinner. They told me that babies had been known to die from infected diaper rash (yeah, in third-world countries), and even though they said Adelle and some other parents had recommended me, I had to assure them about six times that I was good at keeping hind ends clean. They showed me where the wipes and lotions and Luvs were. They showed me how to turn on the baby monitor over the crib. They showed me the bottles of breast milk the mother had pumped and left in the fridge, and how to warm them, and mentioned there was more in the freezer just in case. They cuddled the baby and hoped he wouldn't miss them, then handed him over to me and practically ran out the door.

Of course he started bawling the instant they left, because they expected him to. Babies pick up on that sort of thing. I walked around with him and told him it was okay and patted him for a while, then tried giving him a bottle, but no way would he quiet down. So I packed a diaper bag and put him in his stroller with his Winnie-the-Pooh blanket and took him out for a walk. As soon as I got him out of the house, he stopped crying and started looking around, sucking his fingers and watching the world go by. Okay, good. It was a nice-enough neighborhood with some maple trees, and a comfortable summer evening with just enough breeze to keep the mosquitoes away, and still early enough so there was plenty of golden sundown light left. I'd walk him until he fell asleep.

Only he didn't fall asleep. And I was afraid if I took him back into the house, he'd start screaming again. So I walked him. And walked, and walked some more, exploring streets I hadn't seen before, actually feeling kind of good.

I never in a thousand years expected to meet up with anybody I knew.

But, rock my socks, straight down the sidewalk headed toward me like I'd arranged it came Mason, walking his dog.

Too close to avoid. Otherwise I would have ducked him.

I know it doesn't make sense; but even though I wanted to talk to somebody, I still would have run away if I could.

When he said, "Hey, hi," in that velvety voice of his, I gripped the stroller handles, and the baby started to cry as if my panic had zapped him.

Mason crouched in front of the baby and said, "Hark, it's a rug rat," in such a kindly, insulting way that the baby stopped crying and just stared. There was something about Mason—maybe just weirdness, or maybe a secret in his brown eyes, which he rolled from the baby to me and back again, saying, "Well, well, who would have known."

"I'm just babysitting him, dweeb. He's not mine." I grinned, glad to see him. "You walking Strudel?"

"Merciful heavens, no. What ever gave you such an idea?"

My turn to roll my eyes.

The baby whimpered. I pushed the stroller forward to hush him up, and Mason and the dog turned to walk beside me.

"So, how are you doing?" asked Mason after we'd gone a block in silence.

"Do you really want to know?"

"Of course I really want to know."

I mumbled, "I'm on, like, page six of those papers. It's taking me a while." Even though I really needed to talk with him, I still felt like arguing with him, like it was his fault for giving me the papers in the first place. "Mason, if you think it's so important for somebody to call my mom, why didn't you just go ahead and do it?"

He blinked, and I remembered Adelle hinting that he was illegal. His parents probably kept a real low profile, and he was supposed to do the same, not call attention to himself in any way. But he didn't say that, just lobbed the problem right back to me. "Because I think you should."

"Why?"

"That's a no-brainer. She's your mom, for gosh sake."

"Dad says she's a slut."

"She doesn't look like a slut to me."

"Now that's dumb. How can you tell?"

"Listen, Sherlock Holmes could tell a person's profession just by looking, right? Especially slut. That's a very distinctive look."

He tried to keep it light, but I knew what he meant. I also suspected he was right, but I still said, "You think you're Sherlock Holmes?"

"It doesn't take a detective to tell which way the wind is blowing."

"Huh?"

"Never mind. Mixed metaphor. What specifically does your dad say about your mom?"

So as we walked along with Strudel trotting by Mason's side, I told him some of Dad's stories. As many as I could in the time it took to push the stroller back to the right house.

You'd think I would have been embarrassed, talking that kind of dirt, but it came out like a mud slide. Phone sex, karaoke bars, or biker bars or whatever, skinny-dipping, Mom with two guys at once, the whole hairy enchilada.

When I was finished Mason said in a matter-of-fact way, "I think your dad is projecting."

"*Huh?*"

"Projecting. Like, he's saying your mom did things that really *he* wishes women would do for him. Those sound like male fantasies to me."

"No way!"

"Yes way."

"You qualified as a shrink or something?"

"Hey, I took a psych class, and I'm qualified as a male, believe it or not. Did you know a normal teenage boy thinks about sex on the average of every eight minutes?"

"Jeez. I hope you're not normal."

Mason just smiled. We were already back to the house where I was babysitting, standing on the front walk while Strudel sniffed the baby and the baby stared at Strudel.

"I have a few magazines hidden under my mattress," Mason said.

"So does my brother." And for the first time in my life, I wondered what my father hid under *his* mattress. Like, maybe there was more than one reason why he kept his door padlocked.

"You all right?" Mason asked.

"No." Damn, why did he have to notice? He saw too much, knew too much; he was too damn smart. All of a sudden I felt like everything was his fault, and I wanted to get even. "Tell me something. How did you get your job at the library if you're an illegal alien?"

I felt a heartbeat or two of startled silence before he answered, very low, "I'm not. I was born here. But my parents . . . I don't know who told you, but please don't say anything to anybody."

"How long have they been here?"

"In this town?"

"In America."

"Nearly twenty years."

"How'd they get in?"

"One-year visa. But they couldn't go home again."

"Why not?"

"Nunya, Miss Sherlock." None of my business, he meant, though he said it very gently.

Well, he sure knew all of *my* business. I didn't shut up. "Where would home be if they had to go back?"

I expected him to say nunya again, but he said something quieter and darker. "It's a place that's run by people who make the Mafia look like this little baby boy here."

"So you're protecting your parents."

"Listen, if we got separated it would kill them. That's why I think your mother—"

"But I'm protecting my father."

Just then the baby started to cry. I rolled the stroller back and forth, but he just yelled louder. Hungry.

As I was getting his bottle out, Mason said, "I better leave before the rug rat's parents get back."

Sure, like he was really thinking of me and my babysitting career? He was running away from the conversation, that's all. But off he went before I could tell him so, or yell good-bye, or anything.

I went back inside the house, turned the lights on, fed the baby, burped him, changed his diaper, zipped him into his warm nightie, cuddled him—he was a really sweet baby—and rocked him to sleep, taking all the time in the world because I didn't want to think, and it felt good to hold him. Finally I put him in his crib, on his back the way his mother had told me. She was worried that if he slept on his tummy, he might get SIDS.

His mother. So all about her baby.

Had my mom been like that about me when I was little?

Mom. She was one of the things I was trying not to think about.

8

I WAS FIFTEEN YEARS, FIVE months, and nine days old by the time I finished reading the printouts.

The part about Dad showed a picture of a man with a beard who might as well have been a stranger. It said Daddy had been a used-car dealer, was "engaging in manner and appearance," was "likely to seek employment in automotive sales," and had been granted shared custody of his children after the divorce but had failed to return the children to their mother after his first weekend with them.

It was like he couldn't wait to get us away from Mom. Was she really a slut? Or was he just trying to hurt her because he was angry at her about the divorce?

"The father is in legal violation of a child custody order, and warrants for his arrest have been issued in several states."

That was it. End of story.

Except now it was up to me to decide how to really end the story.

I stood up and shoved the papers into their hiding place under my mattress, but then I just lay down on the bed and stared at the tiles coming loose from the ceiling. I felt like I could never move again, yet after a few minutes I couldn't stand to just lie there, either. I jumped up, stumbled down the stairs, and rushed out of the house with no idea where I was going.

Funny thing, eventually I found myself on Butternut Street.

It was clear across town, so by the time I got there, I was tired and calmer.

My father was a criminal. And a con artist, and I felt pretty sure he'd lied to me for years. I was pissed at him because now I had no idea what my mom was really like.

Yet it felt awful to be mad at him, because he was my Daddy and I loved him. He might not be perfect, but he loved us. He kind of loved Brian one way and me a different way, but he loved us both.

But . . . what about Mom? How did it feel to have your kids taken away? Okay, she probably absolutely hated Daddy, which meant she probably wanted him in jail. But still, didn't she have a right to know her son and her daughter were okay, and where we were, and stuff?

Had she missed us? Did she *still* miss us?

What if I phoned her? What would she say? Would she—would she cry? I felt all achy hot at the thought.

But what if she found out I was fat, and she didn't like me?

And what if she traced the call? I mean, who could blame her if she sent the police to arrest Daddy?

God, oh, God, I needed—

There. Mason's house, or more of a shack really, a shoe-box shape with faded pink vinyl siding peeling off. I could tell it was the right place because out front on a patch of lawn that was more dirt than grass lay Strudel, sunning herself.

When she saw me, she lifted her head, wagged her tail, and woofed to announce me.

Immediately I wished my whole fat body could just disappear. Jeez, what the heck was I doing there? Mason was probably at the library, working. I turned to kazoomba out of there—

"Sherica," called a warm, soft voice.

Sherica. My very own name. It stopped me in my tracks.

I turned around to see Mason coming out the door, telling a couple of giggling little kids behind him, "Nunya, brats. Get back in the house." They did, and he walked over to where I was kind of rooted just outside his yard. He was just a skinny nerd with a shy smile, but I could have hugged him. Okay, because his family was in the country illegally, he couldn't call the cops, so I could trust him—but I think I would have trusted him anyway.

"Carpet creepers," he said happily as he looked over his shoulder to check on his brother and sister. "Curtain climbers." When he turned back to me, his eyes went straight to my face and his quiet smile took me in. "Sherica, you okay?"

I think it was because of his great voice, like he was a doctor or a hypnotist or something, that I was able to say, "I need help."

I don't remember exactly what I said as we sat at Mason's kitchen table. We couldn't go anywhere because he was babysitting the "cognitive aliens," as he called his younger brother and sister. I just know I babbled everything that was on my mind in no logical order, and it would take a genius to figure out what I was talking about. But that's what Mason was, a genius. He barely said a word, just listened and nodded and brought me a glass of ice water. After I don't know how long, I guess I slowed down, and Mason said, of all things, "I'd offer you some oatmeal cookies or something—"

"I'm sick of cookies!" Where the heck had that come from?

"Just as well," Mason remarked, "because the cognitive aliens can smell them from a block away, and they'd be so all over us."

All of a sudden the babysitter in me kicked in. "Where are the kids?"

"Backyard. I can hear them on the swing. Its chains need oil. It sounds like a soul in torture."

Which was kind of what I felt like, but I laughed and stood up to look out the kitchen window at the kids on the rusty old swing set. Geez, I remembered a swing set like that from back when—Mom had probably stood at a window like this one, over the sink. With those short curtains, like lace or something. These weren't lace, just cheap cotton, but they were all ruffled. Dad and Brian hated ruffles. There were plastic sun catchers hanging in this window, butterflies and stuff, and I wondered whether Mom liked that kind of thing the way I did. I wanted to grab one and take it home with me. Whenever I was in somebody's house babysitting, I felt that way, like I wanted to pocket something so I'd have at least a little bit of whatever it was that made other people's houses real homes. I never actually swiped anything, but I wanted to.

"I like your house," I told Mason.

"Really?" He sounded surprised, but let it go because he was looking around for something. Which turned out to be a pen and some paper, the cheap kind they give out in school. He looked at me—his eyes weren't just plain brown, really, but sort of flecked with calm light, like, forest brown. He said, "Sherica, let's try to sort this mess out. Like, make a list. Okay?"

I nodded. We sat at the table.

"Okay. So what's number one? The problem that bothers you the most?"

That was a no-brainer. "I can't do anything that might get Daddy put in jail."

Without any kind of reaction, he wrote it down, then asked, "Then what's number two?"

"Um, Mom. Even if she is a slut like Daddy says, she still has a right to know where her kids are."

He wrote down, "Mom has a right to her kids," then asked, "Number three?"

"Brian. My brother. I need to talk with him about all this, but last time I tried, he hit me."

He kind of stiffened; but he wrote down, "Brian," then asked, "Number four?"

"Just—to figure out what to do so nobody gets hurt. If I phone Mom, she might tell the cops; and if they can find out where the call came from, Daddy might get arrested. If Daddy gets in trouble, Brian will just about die, because he's so all about Dad, and I don't think he gives a crap about Mom. But Mom needs—"

Mason didn't write anything, and for the first time he interrupted. "Sherica. Wait a minute. What do you mean, do it 'so nobody gets hurt'?"

I blinked at him. "Just what I said!"

"But somebody already got hurt," Mason said.

"Yeah, Mom, I guess, but she's been living with it for ten years, so—"

"Sherica," Mason cut me off again, "who is the person who is really suffering right now, the person with her whole future at stake? You haven't even mentioned her."

I had no idea what he was talking about. I just stared at him, and he stared back so intently you'd think *his* life depended on the answer.

When I didn't say anything, he demanded almost as if he was angry, "Aren't you somebody?"

"Huh?"

"You want to do things so nobody gets hurt. Are you nobody?"

If I'd been standing up, I think I would have fallen over, that's how it felt when I finally realized what he meant. I felt my face like, faint and let go of my jaw. My mouth sagged open.

When Mason saw me get it, he smiled. But at the same time, he grumbled, "Daddy this, Mom that, Brian the other, brother schmother." With quick strong strokes he wrote something on the paper.

"There's your list," he said, handing it over to me.

At the top, before anything else, he had put in capital letters, WHAT'S BEST FOR SHERICA?

9

"I AM SOMEBODY," I WHISPERED to myself as I walked back to my end of town. "I *am* somebody," I said over and over because the aching, hungry, hollow feeling couldn't get enough of this treat that was better than chocolate, better than jelly donuts, better than strawberry ice cream or four-cheese pizza or any kind of cookies ever invented. "I am somebody. I am me." How, when, *why* had I forgotten? Was it because of all the different, dumb, fattening names? "I am Sherica."

When I got back to the rental house, I ran, I mean actually ran, up the stairs to shut myself in my room and get the papers out from under my mattress.

"I am Sherica. Sherica Suloff."

I studied the two pictures of myself, the cute little kindergartener and the bright-and-smiling teenager I should be if things had been different. But maybe things *could* be different.

What's best for Sherica?

I had no idea. I had never thought about what I needed, or what I wanted, other than funky earrings. Or—

Footsteps pounded up the stairs. Brian was home.

I *so* wasn't ready to let him in on things yet. I shoved the papers under my pillow before Brian tried to push my door open. "What the hell!" he screamed when the latch hook stopped him. "You big fat blob, open up!"

Kind of automatically I stood up and started toward the door, but then I thought *I am somebody*, and I stopped. Through the crack in the door I said to him, "This is my room."

"Listen, land whale—"

"If you stop yelling, and call me by my right name, I might let you in."

He rolled his eyes. "I *so* beg your pardon, Pattyfatty-cake."

"No. My real name, Brian."

"I told you not to go there!" *That* was what scared him. His face turned so Neanderthal he scared me. I stepped back like he might hit me with a club. "And anytime I want to get into this room, I can bust this door right down!" Which was true; he was strong enough to come through like an SUV. "What have you got yourself locked in there for? I'm telling Dad!"

I took a deep breath and told myself *I am Sherica* before I answered. "Go ahead. Tell him whatever you want. Get him all upset and hurt, like I've been careful not to."

The way Brian blinked, I knew I'd won, kind of. But only for today. I needed to decide *soon* what to do.

The two kids I babysat that night were scribbling with crayons. Their mom had bought them the biggest Crayola box and a thick pad of art paper. Usually I would have let them draw while I watched TV, but something made me sit down at the table with them. I hadn't done anything like that since I was in elementary school, but that night I colored like my life depended on it. Not just grabbing any old crayon, either. Even though I didn't know what I was trying to draw, I needed exactly the right colors, teal and indigo and silver gray and a dark, dark blue called Outer Space. I needed to scrub the darkness across the paper in long swooping strokes kind of like ocean waves at night or clouds blown in a high wind or something.

"What are you drawing?" one of the kids asked after I'd filled about four sheets of paper this way.

"I don't know. Is it okay if I do one more?"

"Sure."

This time some white curved shapes took form in the dark, flowing water, stormy sky, whatever.

"That's nice," one of the kids said. "Can you show me how to draw a sailboat like that?"

I blinked because I don't know a thing about sailboats, and we'd never lived near the seashore or a lake or anything like that; but there it was, a boat with its sail billowing on its tall mast. It wasn't floating on water so much as soaring like a white bird in a dark sky, a bride bird veiled in gray mist and midnight blue. It was weird, but the weirdest thing was the way it made me feel. Real sure of myself. Like I'd been doing this every day of my life, I reached out and with my fingernail I etched long, strong, straight lines of white into the darkness, rays widening like opened arms as they reached out for the sailboat.

A searchlight beam.

Lighthouse, I mean. Faintly, like catching just a whiff of saltwater, I seemed to remember . . . Maybe I *had* visited the sea once. Sometime. Before.

I took that crayon drawing home with me and put it in my room. I didn't hide it. I taped it to the wall.

A couple of days later, I began negotiations to meet with Brian.

Seriously. When I woke up that morning, I felt ready to arrange a conference. I waited until Daddy left for work. Brian was still munching on his super-jock cereal. I sat down across from him and said, "I want to talk with you sometime when you can listen and not yell at me." Real matter-of-fact. "You say when."

"Oh, yeah? What do you want to talk about?"

I stayed calm, quiet. "About Mom."

He spewed cereal and milk as he lunged from his chair, yelling predictably, "What did I tell you about that?"

I stood up, too, but only to walk away. "Let me know when you're ready to have a conversation."

"When pigs like you fly!" he yelled after me.

I didn't answer, just trotted upstairs; and it occurred to me that, if I was as fat as my brother said, then how could I walk clear across town and back without having a heart attack or something? How could I run up the stairs without getting out of breath?

I went into my room, but I didn't latch the door. I just pulled the papers out from under my mattress. Yeah, I was still keeping them in that stupid hiding place under the mattress because I think I'd been kind of hoping my brother would go looking for them and find them himself so I wouldn't have to do this.

But he hadn't.

So I took them into his room and laid them on his bed.

Then I walked back downstairs and out of the house. I didn't feel much hope because he and Dad—the way they were. . . . Still, if I didn't give him a chance, I would always wonder.

I spent all day just wandering around, or in the public library—Mason wasn't there—or with Adelle at the hardware store. Between customers Adelle was painting ceramic cats. "Tortoiseshell," she explained, "which is brown and gold, or calico, which is the same thing plus white. Got to get the spots right, kind of divided down the middle of the cat. Did you know only female cats can be calico?"

Nope, I didn't know that. There was a lot I didn't know.

"And those orange tabbies, they're mostly all male."

I looked at the tabby cats and beagle dogs and all the other ceramic stuff on her shelves, lighthouses and old schoolhouses and grandmas in rocking chairs and little kids holding kittens or puppies, and pinto ponies and contented cows and ducks in a row, which mine definitely were not. I wondered whether Mom liked ducks, or cows, or animals in general, real ones or hand-painted cuties. I wondered whether she collected anything, like maybe hedgehogs.

I didn't want to go back to the rental house, but I felt like I had to see how Brian was, now that he'd had time to explode and calm down some. I figured the minute he saw me he'd start yelling and swearing at me.

But he didn't. It wasn't the way I expected at all. I walked into the house, and there he sat on the sofa in front of the TV; but it was turned off, and he was watching the empty screen. He didn't say a word. He turned his face away from me, but I caught a glimpse of his expression. It was sort of the way people looked after 9/11.

I let him alone. Actually I went into the kitchen and started fixing macaroni and cheese, one of his favorites.

Dad breezed in at about his usual time. "Hi, Blondie!" He hugged me with one arm, pulling off his necktie with his other hand. "Cooking supper? What got into you?"

"Nothing."

"Aren't you going to ask me how my day was?"

"How was your day?"

"I got Associate of the Month, that was how! Top sales. And a raise. When I get my paycheck, we'll go out to Burger King to celebrate, buy you a Whopper. What do you say?"

"Whatever," I muttered, but he didn't wait to hear what I would say. He went to get into comfortable clothes, but as he strode through the living room, he stopped like he'd run into a brick wall. "Hey, big guy, what's the matter?"

No answer.

"You look like you got hit by a bomb, son."

Huh. I'd been looking the same way for, what, weeks now? But Dad had never noticed.

"Listen, whatever it is, it can't be that bad." I heard the sofa creak as Daddy sat down next to Brian. "Tell your old father, what's wrong?"

"Nothing," Brian said, but Dad must have been real worried because he kept asking questions. "Problems with soccer?"

"No, Dad."

"Your girl giving you a hard time?"

"I don't have a girlfriend."

"The heck you don't. You have half the girls in town, as usual. Come on, tell me." Dad's voice lowered. "You got one of them in trouble, is that it?"

"Sure, right, that's it!" All of a sudden Brian was yelling. "Like all I do—"

"Well, if that's not it, just tell me! What is it?"

"Nothing! Let me alone." I heard Brian run up the stairs to his room and slam the door. After a minute Dad came back into the kitchen where I was mixing chopped green peppers into the macaroni and cheese.

He asked, "Blondie, do you know what's bothering your brother?"

"No," I lied. My voice came out real hard. "It's just one of his moods."

10

FOR THE NEXT THREE DAYS, Brian barely said hi to Dad, and he wouldn't talk to me at all or even look at me. I don't think he was giving me the silent treatment, not really; I think he just couldn't deal. But that didn't change the way it made me feel. Brian upset. Dad worrying about Brian.

My brother and my dad. My dad and my brother.

What's best for Sherica?

Even though I had no more papers to read, I still spent a lot of time in my room. And the more I looked at my silver-sailboat-in-the-darkness drawing, the more it seemed to be trying to tell me what I needed.

I started daydreaming about how Mom was going to rescue me. Mom was one hundred percent exactly the opposite of what Daddy said about her; she was a hero. She was strong, athletic, and she did things. She knew how to ride horses and sail boats, things like that. She was brave, and not just physically. She stood up for what was right and wouldn't let anybody take advantage of anybody else. Like, she went out at night with a big halogen flashlight to find homeless people and help them. If a little girl got lost in the woods, Mom would find her. She took care of starving cats and stray dogs, too. She was way beautiful, but she didn't care about men at all. She was practically a virgin; like, she'd had sex once to have Brian and once to have me, then quit. And now she just wanted to make the world a better place. She was strong inside as well as outside. She had heart. She cared about everybody. Even fat teenage girls. And the minute she heard about me, she would . . . well, I tried various scenarios. She would fly in on a private jet—but no, there was no airport. Okay, a helicopter, a big one, and she'd tell Daddy it was *not right* to steal little girls away from their mothers. She would give him a glare that would shut him up instantly if he made any trouble, and she would hug me and—and what? Stay with me? Buy us a house of our own?

Well, she'd do something, anyway.

Unlike certain other people. Like my brother. He was never going to do anything.

Well, what was it that I hoped he'd do, anyway? Understand me? Back me up?

Help me get away?

Help me go back to Mom?

When those words hit it must have been three o'clock in the morning, but I sat straight up in bed, with my heart pounding. At that moment I first admitted to myself what I wanted to do. I could think it now, maybe I could say it, and maybe I could even do it if Brian would—*If Brian would come with me.*

Oh, if only he would! Sure, he was a jerk sometimes, but he was bigger, and older, and stronger, and I would feel safer with him, and—and he was my brother. I didn't want to leave *everything* behind.

But maybe a bigger truth was that if Brian went along with me, I wouldn't have to wonder and worry whether I was doing the right thing. I wouldn't have to make the whole decision. I wouldn't have to go on my own.

Really, I didn't feel like I would ever be strong enough to do that.

Four days went by. Five.

I kept daydreaming, only now it was more like Brian and I rescued Mom. All dressed in black she was shut in a narrow, dark house, just waiting to die when Brian and I showed up. When Mom saw us she cried so hard she fainted, and Brian gently picked her up—

Yeah, right.

In my real-life thinking, I'd pretty much given up on Brian when on day six he came into the kitchen, saying, "Miss a bite, Blimp. Come on if you want to talk." I was just eating a tuna sandwich, for gosh sake, my lunch, but I let it pass. Without a word I got up to follow him.

I couldn't have said anything if I'd wanted to. Now I knew what people meant when they said their heart was in their throat.

Even though Dad would not be home until suppertime, we went upstairs and into my bedroom. Brian brought the computer printouts from his room, then hooked my door latch. We sat on opposite ends of my bed, and Brian tossed the papers down halfway between us.

"I suppose you want these back," he said in kind of a low voice. "You don't know how many times I nearly tore them up."

I kept myself from pointing out that I could have replaced them because he was being okay in his way. I guess it would be hard for anybody except me to tell the difference, but he wasn't actually being a jerk. He was just upset and telling me the truth about it. I mean, he'd made himself a comfortable world, big strong jock, Dad's buddy, everything's okay, and I had laid an earthquake on him.

"So what's your point?" he asked, his voice still soft but his hand rough, shoving the papers toward me. "What do you want me to *do*?"

Why did Brian always think I wanted him to do something, when usually all I wanted was just to talk, share, be friends? This time, yeah, I wanted him to do something, but no way was he ready. So I said softly, "Tell me about Mom."

"What?" He wasn't expecting that, and the surprise knocked some of the edge off him.

"You're older," I explained. "You probably remember more. Tell me what she was like."

"I've told you a thousand times, she was a slut."

"That's what Dad says. But what do you actually remember?"

"Are you calling Dad a liar?"

I just looked at him, and after a minute he had to look away.

"I'll go first," I said. "I remember Mom used to make zebra cakes for our birthdays. White frosting with chocolate stripes. Do you remember that?"

He nodded, still not looking at me.

I tried again. "I remember she had superhero Band–Aids."

"Yeah, you were always falling off the swing, and she was always making a fuss over you," he muttered.

"I don't suppose anybody ever *pushed* me off the swing," I remarked.

He smiled. Just for a second, but I saw it. And my heart pounded yes, yes! If I could get him to bypass all the stuff Dad had put in his brain, and remember Mom with his heart, then maybe . . . maybe he would help me, go along with me, maybe even make the phone call for both of us so it wouldn't be all my fault if anything bad happened to Dad.

Looking out the window like I was just thinking aloud, not really asking him, I said, "What was in the backyard besides the swing set?"

"Sprinkler. When it was hot, she'd let us—" Brian stopped and swallowed hard.

That made *me* remember. It was the freakiest feeling when the memory came, like sailing out of a mist in my mind. I whispered, "She bought us squirt guns. A yellow one for me and a red one for you."

"Stop it." Brian's voice sounded buzzy tight like the strings on an electric guitar. "Stop it right now. What the hell do you want?"

Maybe I should have told him the truth right then, but I didn't. There was something else on my mind. I took a deep breath. "I want to know, do you remember the guy on the motorcycle?"

"No."

"Or the one with the ponytail?"

"No. Don't, Sherica."

Talk about electric. A power surge warmed me all over when he said that, when he called me Sherica. But I tried not to show how I felt.

I said quietly, "I just need to know. That's all."

Actually, I didn't expect him to remember anything about any men at all, the way I had fantasized about Mom like a princess in a tower or something. So it hit me in the gut when Brian muttered, "There was this guy who hung around. Kept bringing me action figures. And Barbie doll stuff for you."

"I don't remember that."

"Yeah, well, why would you? I think he was Mom's boyfriend. I think he was the reason she and Dad split up."

I have to admit I'm the one who raised my voice first. "You don't know that! Maybe *Dad* did something to—"

"You're always against Dad!"

"I'm just trying to say—"

"*Shut up!*" Brian shot to his feet. He grabbed the computer printouts and shook them at me. "All this is just so Mom can get back at Dad."

"It is not! She wants us!"

"You don't know that! Dad takes care of us!"

"Dad takes care of *you*!" I clutched at the papers to take them away from him. They tore. Between the two of us, we ripped Mom's photo in half. We ripped everything in half.

"Now look what you did!" I yelled.

"Me! Look what *you're* trying to do!" My brother acted mindless most of the time, but in some important ways he was really smart. Too smart. "What the hell is this thing?" he demanded, and he rammed over to my wall, tore down my drawing of the sailboat and searchlight, and ripped it into little bits. He kept ripping it smaller and smaller, like confetti, while he shouted at me, "Whatever you're thinking in that stupid fat head of yours, forget it! You're not going anywhere or doing anything and if you try to, I'm telling Dad."

And Dad would pack us both up and move us somewhere else and change our names and the color of our hair and probably lock me in an attic and who cared?

"Is that all you can think about!" I screamed back. "Dad?"

There was this sudden, freaky silence, as I looked at the bits of my sailboat picture littering the floor. What the heck had I been thinking? Searchlights weren't for finding lost kids. Searchlights spotted targets to shoot down. Just like what my brother was doing to me. Brian, standing there and staring at me in the weirdest way, as if we weren't speaking the same language.

"Dad's the *man*," he declared, like he was telling me something he shouldn't have to explain.

"What you mean," I shot back, "is that you're Daddy's shadow."

"I am not! I'm his son. We're family. You just don't get it, do you? What's the matter with you?"

And I couldn't answer him. I couldn't put it in words, but I could feel it. He was way more Dad's son than he was my brother. And he and Daddy were way more family than the three of us were. He was okay being Dad's son; he didn't have to be Brian to be somebody.

I mumbled, "You're the one who just doesn't get it."

"Get what?"

"What about—" I wanted to say *what about me*, but I knew I didn't count. "What about Mom?"

"Jeez, what's your problem? Who cares about her?" He started to storm out, but at the door he turned to stare at me with narrow eyes. "I'm warning you. Don't do anything stupid. Mom doesn't want you. Who do you think you *are?*"

And I wanted to say I was Sherica, but somehow I couldn't anymore.

Brian watched me for a minute, then slammed the door and left me shut in my room.

I ripped what was left of the printout papers into confetti bits, too. I ripped up all the phone numbers, ripped up what was left of the photograph of my mother, everything. Tore them up into tiny shreds that fell to the floor and laid there like bodies after a battle, like they were all that was left of Sherica.

11

"I CAN'T DO IT," I told Mason in a whisper because we were in the library. He was behind the desk, working, checking in a stack of books. I'd been dropping by to talk with him after work some days, but I shouldn't have been there when I might get him in trouble with his boss. I shouldn't have been there or anywhere when I probably looked as bad as I felt, but I really needed to talk to him.

"Brian won't go with me," I whispered. "And I can't do it all by myself. I just can't."

With those gold-flecked, wise brown eyes of his, Mason studied me. "Brian? Your brother? Are you two close?"

I kind of hiccupped, almost a laugh. "Hardly!"

Mason stood up to put the books on a cart, then faced me, leaning toward me over the counter. In a low tone he asked, "What happens to Brian if you get a life?"

"Nothing. But he's probably right about Mom. He said she had a boyfriend." And boy, was I having trouble with that.

"Can't a normal adult woman have a boyfriend if her marriage is—"

"Brian says she blew the marriage. Then Dad took us kids, and now she just wants to get back at Dad. She doesn't really care about getting us kids back." I forgot to whisper. "Especially not me. She might want her cute little girl back, but not a big, fat cow of a teenager."

"Don't talk about yourself like that!" Mason was forgetting to whisper, too. "You never really had a mom, so you don't understand. Moms don't stop caring—"

"So, what if she still hates Dad? What if all she wants is to put Daddy in jail?"

"You'd rather be in jail yourself?"

I didn't understand what he was saying. "I'm okay. I'm fine. Everything can just stay the way it is."

Mason kept shaking his head. "It's not right. Parents should protect children, not the other way around."

"You should talk about children protecting their parents," I shot back.

"Shhh." Shock as if I'd hit him flashed in his eyes, making me wish I'd never said it; and darn, just at that moment here came his boss out of her back office. "That's different," he muttered, turning away from me, putting the books in order on the cart as if his life depended on it. "Listen, you better go."

"I'm sorry," I whispered.

"Don't sorry me. Take care of *yourself*."

"But I'm okay."

"*Sure* you are."

"I'm fine!"

He didn't look up or say anything. His boss walked behind the desk.

I left.

I *was* fine, I told myself, heading kazoomba down the sidewalk with my flip-flops flapping. Everything was okay now that I'd made up my mind to stay. Nothing had to change.

Fine.

Good. No trouble, no problem.

So why did I feel so awful?

A couple of days went by, and I didn't feel any better. I hung around with Adelle, and I guess she could see I was bummed because she tried talking with me about making plans for school, like, maybe I could join 4–H or something, and where the best places were to get new clothes. Without even mentioning bras she offered to take me shopping, to drive me around in her car, which was really nice of her. And I had a lot of babysitting money saved up and nothing to use it for now, so why not? We arranged to go to the mall on Saturday, after the hardware store closed.

But I kind of felt worse instead of better because school meant being in the same building as Mason, and I'd really let him down. I tried to tell myself that maybe by the time school started, this whole stupid thing would be, like, ancient history, and I'd be able to be Mason's friend again. I figured that being such a nerd, even though he was being the best nerd he could be, still, maybe he could use a friend, even if she was a land whale.

I replaced my Mom daydreams with Mason ones. I imagined some bully trying to knock Mason's books onto the floor while I, the much-scorned obese new student, knocked the bully to the floor instead and sat on him. If I had to be a weight case, well, I'd weigh in. For the good guys. See, I had a secret identity, Sherica rhymed with America, and I did things to protect other people's freedom, just not my own. I defended the misfits, and popular kids who tried to call me a fat pig were going to learn to refer to me as Super Sow. Yeah!

Yeah, right.

Mason had never mocked me. I was doing it to myself.

I still felt bad about mentioning his parents in the library. And maybe he felt bad about making me leave.

If I wanted to keep being friends, I'd better go talk to him.

Yet I didn't want to face him. I felt like I'd let him down.

And I was so tired and, like beat up, sore all over. I just couldn't get myself moving to do *anything*. Aside from watching Adelle paint ceramic caterpillars, I mostly just laid in bed.

But the day after Adelle and I talked about shopping, I rolled over, sat up, got out of bed, found a notebook, and wrote a letter.

Dear Mason,
I never thanked you for everything you tried to do for me. THANK YOU, even though it didn't work out the way you wanted. Nobody else has ever done so much for me. Printing all the papers and getting them to me in such a smart, gutsy way and especially asking me WHAT'S BEST FOR SHERICA? I guess staying with my father and my brother is not best, but it's safe, and not really bad, just kind of fattening. And for all I know, my mother might be way worse. I guess it's stupid me writing you this letter, but for some reason I don't have the guts to face you.

My handwriting showed that; it wobbled. Like me, my handwriting is round and oversized, and now it was unsteady, too.

> Thank you, Mason, for trying to
> help me even though I'm not
> worth it.
> Sincerely,
> Sh—

But something stopped me. I couldn't write my real name.

And I wanted to, darn it. This one last time. I looked at what I had written:

> Thank you, Mason, for trying
> to help me, even though I'm not
> worth it.

I stared at the last six words. They felt wrong. Even though I'd meant them when I wrote them, they seemed not true, not if I was Mason's friend. And not if I was Sherica.

I erased, leaving:

> Thank you, Mason, for trying to
> help me.

and then I could sign my name.

> Sincerely,
> Sherica

There.

I put this in an envelope with Mason's name on it, but I didn't know his exact address. I washed my face, combed my hair, stuck out my tongue at myself in the mirror, then thumped downstairs and headed off with my letter, walking to Butternut Street, on the hottest, muggiest, most annoying and miserable day all summer. Mason would be working in a nice air-conditioned library. But what if he *was* home? Walking through the sweaty heat with the cicadas chittering in the browning-out trees, I decided I wouldn't knock on the door of his house; I would leave my letter in the Kuftas' mailbox.

There. Mason's house with pink siding peeling like sunburn, but—

But no ruffled curtains in the windows.

Nothing at all in the windows. No sun-catchers. No lights. No life.

No noodle-haired Strudel on the patch of lawn. Instead, a FOR RENT sign.

In the gravel driveway a gray pickup truck.

Front door hanging open.

Woman who looked like a toad in an orange sweatshirt coming out, lugging a box.

Zapped by what I was seeing, shocked rigid with my mouth open, I got myself moving when I saw her and ran to her. "Mrs. Kufta?" I demanded because I still didn't want to believe.

"Hell, no," she said, stopping just long enough to glare

at me before she thumped the box into the pickup. "I'm their landlord."

"Where are the Kuftas?"

"You and me and a lot of other people would like to know! Snuck off in the middle of the night. Owe me a month's rent, and their security deposit doesn't begin to cover the mess they left."

"Why? When? Where'd they go?"

She didn't pay any attention. I was just a body to complain to as she headed back into the house. ". . . crappy old clothes and busted-up toys and all sorts of junk I got to get rid of, and the immigration people after me like it's my fault, like I'm supposed to check people's citizenship papers before I rent to them."

I trailed along behind her. Inside, the house was like the brown shell of a cicada, clinging to a tree like something alive, when actually it's totally empty. I'd seen empty rooms often enough, dust and marks and dropped pretzels on the carpet where the furniture used to be, but always when I was the one leaving. Never when I was the one left behind.

"Are they ever *coming back*?" I begged.

"What are you doing in here?" Toad-face turned on me as if she'd just become aware of me. "What are you, some school friend of the kids? No, I kinda doubt they're coming back!"

"Do you know where they—"

"If I knew where they went, I'd be on my way there to collect the rent!" She headed toward me with a garbage bag from the kitchen. "You're in my way. Get out of here." She gave me a look like I was a big slug that had crawled in, leaving a trail of slime. "You're trespassing. This is private property."

I left and didn't even mind the way she talked to me because I had other things to feel bad about.

I would never get to thank Mason.

I would never know what had become of him.

I would never see him again.

My heart hurt. Walking away from his house, I started crying. Mason had been a friend, and probably I'd never see him again, and I couldn't stop crying. I felt like I'd never stop crying. I'd always remember him. Always. And every time I thought of him, I'd get that same pain in my heart—

Then it hit me.

Just as I reached the locust tree on the corner of Butternut Street, it hit me so bull's-eye in my brain that it stopped me in my tracks:

This is how Mom feels.

Only ten thousand times worse.

And in that moment my tears dried up like somebody shut off the faucet because I knew. I knew where my big, hungry heart came from, and it sure wasn't from my father. I knew Mom had a heart like mine. I knew she loved me and would always want me, no matter if I was fat or flat or five or fifteen, no matter what. And I knew what to do. I didn't have to reason it out. I didn't have to convince myself. I just knew it, like knowing sky is up and boats sail in the wind.

12

ALL THE WAY BACK TO the rental house, I strode along with my brain going like Adelle's hands when she painted something, an artist's hands filling in the big picture, the plan, swift and totally sure, taking care of every detail. Never before in my whole life had I thought so quickly, clearly, and well. By the time I'd walked across town, I was ready.

Ready when I walked into the kitchen. There sat Brian at the table, shoveling butter-pecan ice cream into his mouth. I knew I might never see him again, and I felt watery inside; but I just said, "Hey, eating fatso food. That's my job," and I headed past him, up to my room. I took all my babysitting money from where I'd hidden it in an envelope taped to the bottom of a dresser drawer—*not* under the mattress—and I put it into a purse. I don't always carry a purse, but it's not unheard of. So nobody would notice if I used it to take just a few things with me.

Clean underwear. Deodorant. My zit cream. Toothbrush. Photos—for the first time I was sorry I didn't have good photos of Brian and Dad, because Dad didn't allow us to own cameras or take pictures. But I had a few photos that people had given me from school events. I took those. And my library card because I would need it in order to use the computer.

I put on sneakers and grabbed a fleece hoodie.

Then I looked all around my room, but there was not another thing that I wanted or needed to take along.

So I sat down to write the letter.

I didn't let myself fuss over it too much. I wrote it down straight and sure, the way my mind, still working like a quick-fingered artist, told me:

Dear Dad and Brian,
I'm on my way back to Mom. I love you both and I'll never bad-mouth either of you, but the way we've been living is not good for me. I need to be Sherica. So this note is to say good-bye. Brian, if you want to see me again, it's up to you; just pick up the phone. Dad, I'm not judging you, and I am giving you a chance to get away. I'm not going to call the cops, and it'll

take me a few days to get where I'm going, so you have a little time. But when I get there, if Mom asks where I've been, I'll tell her. I won't lie about anything that's happened for the past ten years, but I know you've been the best father to me you could be, considering who you are. I figure Mom's another adult just being who she is, and having a boyfriend doesn't make her a slut. She won't be able to solve all my problems, but she'll be the best mom to me she can be. And a mom is what I need, so I'm going now. I'm sorry for the inconvenience.

Bye,
Sherica

I left this letter on top of the toilet, which sounds really gross but was actually the most practical place I could think of because I knew either Dad or Brian would be sure to find it there. I hoped not too soon. Dad would be home from work in a couple of hours. I wished I'd got started at a more sensible time, like morning, but it was now or never. If I waited until tomorrow, I wouldn't be able to sleep. I'd think too much and might lose my momentum, lose my Sherica, turn into a donut again. No. I had to go.

So I took my purse and headed downstairs. Brian was watching some extreme sports show on TV. I let myself take a long look at him, and I felt like my insides were turning over, but I didn't let myself show it as I walked past him and said, "Bye."

Watching wrestlers try to tear each other apart, Brian didn't look at me, but he did ask, "Where are you going?"

I said, "Where do you think?" knowing he would assume I had a babysitting job, and I headed on out the door. I didn't look back.

The public library was closed when I got there.

I simply could not believe it. The stupid library was closed. I should have guessed it might be because Mason was practically the only employee they had and how were they supposed to stay open without him? I guess my genius mind had missed part of the picture after all.

So now what?

Without the phone numbers my plan wouldn't work. The plan was to hustle my big butt to the bus station, buy an overnight ticket to anywhere, get away from town so my call couldn't be traced back to Daddy and Brian, sleep on the bus to give them till tomorrow sometime, then call Missing & Exploited Children or one of those organizations with an 800 number to get me back to Mom.

But without the phone numbers, if I got on the bus, then how—what—if libraries required cards—and the idea of walking into a strange library, or wandering around a strange town looking for one—what if I got picked up by the cops if they thought I was, like, a runaway?

Which, actually, I was.

When I realized that, I really started to panic. I could think only the worst. What if the cops didn't let me tell them about Mom? Or didn't believe me? *What if they sent me back to Dad?*

Oh my God, I had to go somewhere, do something, fast! Suppose Brian had already found my note. Any minute he might come barreling down the street, hoping to catch me. I had to get out of sight.

Somewhere he'd never think to look for me.

My feet, which seemed to be smarter than my head at that point, already had me running; and just as I thought of going to Handy Hardware, I was already there.

Adelle, who was painting something as usual, glanced up and smiled when I blundered in. "Hello, honey. I haven't seen you for a few days. How is everything?"

"Um, weird." All of a sudden I felt tears stinging my eyes just because she was nice to me. "Do you know where Mason is? I really need to talk with him."

"The Kufta boy?" Adelle lost her smile, looking concerned as she put her paintbrush into water and set aside what she was working on. "Hadn't you heard, sweetie? The Kuftas skipped town, trying to avoid being deported."

"I had heard, but I—" I'd been hoping for a miracle, and I was being a big dumb blob, just like my brother always said, standing right inside the glass door where anybody could see me. I forced myself to move farther into the store.

"Here, honey pie." Adelle patted the seat of a chair next to her, behind the counter. Perfect; nobody passing on the street could see me there. I sat, and she asked, "You have a problem? Is it anything I can help with?"

Trying to hold back tears, I said, "No. Thanks anyway, I—"

I am Sherica.

Adelle asked gently, "The Kufta boy, is that what's upsetting you?"

I am somebody. I am allowed to ask for help. I said, "Yes and no. Not exactly. Adelle, do you have, like, um, a computer? To get on the Internet?"

"Not here at the store, honey. It's at home. What do you need to know?"

Rather than try to explain all about Missing & Exploited Children and 800 numbers and everything, I said it the simplest way I could. "My mother's phone number."

No more beating around the bush. No more strangers, rescue organizations, whatever. I didn't care anymore whether Mom had caller ID or whether she might trace the call. "I want to find my mom."

I saw Adelle's eyes open wide, but she kept her voice as no-problem, as if I'd asked for a glass of water. "Is it in the phone book?"

"I don't know."

"When's the last time you spoke with her, hon?"

"About ten years ago."

Adelle no longer tried to hide her surprise. "Why such a long time?"

I just shook my head.

After puckering her lips for a moment, Adelle tried again. "Where does she live?"

"I don't know whether she's still in Latrobe or not."

"Latrobe?"

"Pennsylvania." Which was quite a distance from here.

Adelle shook her head, blinked, and took a couple of long breaths. Then she reached under the counter and handed me a cordless phone. "Here. Try Information."

I stared at the phone in my hand as if I'd never seen one before.

"Dial four–one–one."

I did; then asked a recorded voice for Latrobe, Pennsylvania; then asked another one for Monica Suloff.

Then waited.

Adelle shoved a pen and paper in front of me.

A real person came on the line. "City and name, please?"

"Latrobe, Pennsylvania. Monica Suloff."

I could feel Adelle sitting next to me, waiting. I could feel my own heart drumming.

The real person said, "Spell the last name, please."

"S–U–L–O–F–F." My voice came out thin because it was hard to breathe, like a python had constricted around my chest. I already knew what was going to happen.

Sure enough. "I show no listing for anyone by that name," the real person said.

I don't remember whether I said thank you before I clicked off. Probably I did. My reflex is to be a polite person.

Adelle didn't say anything at first, but I could imagine all the questions she was keeping herself from asking as she suggested ever so calmly, "Maybe your mother has an unlisted number."

I stared at the phone in my hand. A black phone. Why did so many phones have to be black? I hate that color. It's like doom, or death, or something. I said, "I don't know whether her last name is still Suloff."

"Oh. Perhaps she's remarried?"

"Yeah, or even if she didn't, why would she want to keep the last name of a jerk like my dad?" There, I'd gone and said it, when I'd just promised I'd never bad-mouth him to anybody.

"She divorced him? Maybe she took back her maiden name."

I barely paid attention to what she said, just shook my head, because I was, like, running out of strength. It was like the Sherica in me, which wasn't real strong anyway, was struggling to run a marathon and just about to give up.

"Which," Adelle went on, "should be your maternal grandmother's last name. Did you have a grandma, hon?"

Grandma.

Sherry.

I reared up in my chair with a jolt, staring at—at a white sailboat, of all things. Adelle was painting a little ceramic sailboat that day.

13

"SAYLOR," I WHISPERED.

"Huh?"

"Saylor!" This time I shouted it out loud because of the way it came to me out of the mist, like the memory of the yellow and red squirt guns. Saylor! Mom's mom, Sherry, was Grandma Saylor. When I was little I had thought it meant, like, a sailor on a sailboat. How could I have forgotten?

Or had I forgotten? Who had drawn that picture of a white sailboat? Sherica deep inside me.

I really AM Sherica.

My hands fumbled as I grabbed the phone and called Information again. They didn't have a listing for Sherry Saylor or Monica Saylor, but I knew a lot of women didn't put their first names in the phone book, so I asked for all the Saylors in Latrobe, Pennsylvania. I started trembling as I wrote down the numbers. There were, like, a dozen of them.

My voice shook as I told Adelle, "I'll pay you for the calls."

"No, you most absolutely will not, sweetie pie. Go right ahead. Good luck." She held up both hands to show me her fingers crossed for me.

She actually made me smile as I started dialing.

At the first number I got an answering machine and hung up.

At the second number I got a grumpy man who didn't know any Monica or any Sherry.

But at the third number, a woman's voice said, "Hello?" and that was all it took. I couldn't have told you what Mom's voice sounded like, but my whole body recognized it before my mind could wrap around it, even more than when I saw her photograph. I went weak all over; I couldn't speak. I dropped the phone, but Adelle caught it.

And she spoke into it. "You still there, ma'am? Okay. Please don't hang up."

I sat there, gasping for breath as if somebody had punched me in the stomach.

Adelle said, "Yes, it's very important. Are you Monica Suloff, or, um, Saylor?" She listened, then nodded at me. I started to cry.

Adelle asked her, "Is there somebody there with you,

ma'am? Are you sitting down? Yes. Yes, it is. It's about your daughter." And she handed the phone to me.

I managed to choke out, "M-M-Mom?"

And she tried to say something. I think it was my name, but I couldn't tell for sure because she was crying, too. I couldn't understand a word. But it didn't matter because I did understand what I really needed to: how very, very, truly I was somebody.

Adelle got up and walked away into the tool aisles to give us some privacy; but it wouldn't have mattered because even when we were able to get some words out, we didn't make much sense. I can't remember every word exactly because I felt like a washing machine on the spin cycle, dizzy, sloshy, fragrant clean, and all shook up, but I think it went something like this:

"Mom? Listen, I'm not pretty or anything. I'm fat."

"Sherica! Are you okay?"

"I'm fat."

"Where are you?"

"Mom, does it matter that I'm fat?"

"Of course not! Where *are* you?"

Obviously she didn't have flashing lights or a call tracer or caller ID, or she wouldn't be asking. And I didn't want to lie to her. But at the same time I couldn't tell her the truth because I still felt like Dad needed time to get away, and trying to think how to answer made me start crying again. I choked out, "Mom—did we ever, like—take a vacation—by the seashore?"

"I'm fat, too, Sherica, depending on who's looking."

She wanted me to feel better and that made me feel so good that I bawled so hard I could barely talk. "Mom—I'll call you back—later."

"No, Sherica, don't hang up!"

"I'll call. In a few hours. I promise." All of a sudden I calmed down some. "Mom, there's stuff I gotta do, and you gotta trust me to handle it. Please."

There was a little silence, and then she said, of all things, "We vacationed at Virginia Beach when you were four. Sherica . . . "

"I'm here."

"Sherica, I love you."

"I'll see you soon," I said. "I'll call later today. You trust me?"

"I trust you."

"Okay. Bye for now." I clicked off because I knew I had to get moving before Adelle had too much time to think or ask me questions or tell herself she ought to notify the police. Right now she was waiting on another customer. I left money on the counter, enough for the phone calls plus a ceramic figurine, and I took the little sailboat. She had barely started to paint it, which was good because I wanted it just the way it was, all white. I slipped it into my purse, along with Mom's phone number, and headed for the door. "Thanks, Adelle," I called over my shoulder.

Adelle called back, "Honey, wait! Where are you going?"

"Home," I told her, and that was the truth.

I ran to the bus station, terrified all the way that Dad or Brian or Adelle or the cops would grab me. By the time I got there, I was panting. As I puffed around the corner and kazoombaed—no, that is not a good word—as I trotted into the exit driveway, there was a bus leaving, and I wind-milled my arms to flag it down. The driver gave me an angry look, but he stopped.

As I climbed on he said, "You need to get to Alabama that bad?" It wouldn't have mattered whether he had said Colorado or Wisconsin, just as long as it was miles from here. I told him yes and asked him how much and paid him the cost of the ticket, plus a tip. I knew he was breaking rules for me, but it's amazing what you can get away with when you're determined enough. The bus was only half full, anyway. I slumped into an empty seat, sort of curled up, until we were out of town and on the interstate. Then I sat up straight and breathed and laid my head back with my eyes closed and breathed some more. And slowly I felt myself filling with a kind of fresh air, a sweet new wind.

I was Sherica.

Homeward bound.

When I opened my eyes, everything looked golden. It was sunset. Families were probably sitting down to supper. Funny, I hadn't thought to bring any food with me, not even a pack of donuts, and that was okay. I didn't feel hungry. I mean, not the way I used to.

There was only one thing I wanted.

I looked around at the other people in the bus. A gray-haired guy in a Florida Seminoles hat looked back at me. I moved a couple of seats closer and asked him, "Do you have a cell phone I could use? I'll pay you. I need to call my mother."

He studied me like I was a puzzle; but he said, "No problem," pulling a little folding cell phone out of his pocket and passing it across the bus aisle to me.

Mom answered on the first ring. "Sherica?" She sounded half out of her mind.

"Yeah, it's me, Mom."

"Oh, thank God!"

"Okay, Mom, I can sort of tell you where I am now." I felt my eyes starting to sting. I couldn't keep a little hitch out of my voice, but at least I could talk. "I'm on a bus. I had to get out of town before—" Suddenly I hated what I had to say. I took it slow. "See, Mom, Brian didn't want to come with me. He's real close with Dad. And I, um, I know what Dad did but I"—my voice started to shake—"I don't want him to go to jail."

"That's the last thing on my mind, Sherica, sweetie. I'm just so . . . so overwhelmed . . . where are you?"

"The bus goes to Alabama."

"Where in Alabama? When?"

"Um, just a minute." I looked up and asked the guy who had loaned me the cell phone, "Where are we going, and when do we get there?"

The look on his face was kind of like the look on Adelle's when I'd talked with Mom the first time. But he didn't ask any questions, just pulled a bus schedule out of his front shirt pocket, unfolded it, and started reading it aloud.

Mom interrupted. "Your first stop is Nashville, Tennessee?"

"That's right."

"Sherica, get off at Nashville. Stay at the bus station, and please be safe until I get there. I'll be there. I promise."

"You—what—how—"

"I don't know yet, but *I will be there*." And she echoed what I had said to her earlier. "Trust me?"

"Sure. Yes."

"Okay, sweetie, I want to give you my cell-phone number. Do you have a pen?"

The gray-haired guy did. Mom gave me her cell-phone number, and I wrote it big and bold on my hand.

Mom said, "If you get scared or worried or anything,

call me, okay? Or just call me whenever. I'll see you in a few hours, Sherica honey, and I can't wait. Are you okay?"

"I guess."

"Oh, my God, Sherica, sweetie, I just want to talk, but I've got to get moving. *Nashville.* I'll see you in a few hours, all right?"

"All right. I'll be there. Bye."

Actually, we said good-bye about six times. She told me again that she loved me. I felt lightheaded when we were done. As I handed the cell phone and the pen back to the nice guy across the aisle, he was watching me like I was a really intense movie.

"Thank you," I told him, sounding watery even to myself.

He nodded but didn't say a word.

I took the little ceramic sailboat out of my purse, holding it in both hands. It nestled there like a white dove. It was safe; it didn't need a searchlight. Lighthouse, I mean. Searchlights can be for shooting things down, but lighthouses are for, like, helping. Bringing a lost kid home. Guiding her on her way.

14

NOW IT WAS NIGHTTIME. OUTSIDE the bus, I couldn't see anything to distract myself. It was, like, four hours till Nashville, and I didn't know how I was going to stand it. But at the same time, I was really worn out, and empty in a good way, like, weightless. I kind of zoned out for a while. Maybe I even slept a little, off and on. Then I would sit up; and when the bus passed a light, I would hold up my hand to make sure Mom's cell phone number was still there.

Mom! Would she know me? I didn't see how she possibly could unless I was the only fat teenage girl in the place. Would I recognize her? Would she be older like Adelle with gray hair and loose blue jeans, or would she be, like, not a slut, please no, but made up and with dyed hair? I tried to remember what she looked like in her photograph, but I couldn't remember a thing except the feeling of knowing her. Would I know her that same way in person? Or would I let her walk right past me?

Would I like her?

Would she like me? Would she love me the way she said?

My hands shook as I slipped the ceramic sailboat back into my purse. I felt all swollen inside; my heart was pounding. It was midnight and we weren't supposed to get to Nashville until around one in the morning. No way could I sleep anymore. Ten minutes past midnight . . . fifteen. . . . I took my watch off and put it into my purse so I would stop looking at it.

And it wasn't just a matter of getting to Nashville, either. I felt sure I'd have to wait at the bus station for Mom because no way could she possibly make it to Nashville ahead of me. She had told me to be safe, so I would stay right near the ticket counter. If there was a public phone, I'd call her on her cell to find out where she was and when she would get there. Then I would have to wait. I knew I ought to eat because I was starting to feel shaky. So I would get some peanut butter crackers or something out of a vending machine. They ought to have vending machines. Then I would sit down someplace in a lighted area to eat and wait.

City lights appeared outside the bus now, finally. I leaned forward on the bus seat, hanging on to my purse with both hands, trembling.

"Nashville!" yelled the driver in a bored voice as we pulled into the bus station.

Nashville. I stood up, and the minute I started moving, I felt better. I stopped shaking because I had a plan: first the public phones—no, make that first the restroom; then the public phones; then the vending machines. Striding along I was not even looking around as I walked into the bus station—

Somebody gasped. Or sobbed. My eyes flew to her, standing at the entrance, waiting for me, heading toward me with her arms out, crying, "Sherica? Sherica!"

I can't even begin to describe what she looked like, except a perfect mom, in a T-shirt a lot like mine, and big like me, cushy all over like a pillow on feet. And I can't remember much of the next half hour except hugs and tears and more hugs and her asking me mom-type things, such as, did I need to go to the bathroom? (Yes.) Was I hungry? (Yes.) Was I warm enough? (Yes.) And she kept on saying how beautiful I was. Beautiful. "Like an angel," she said. "Perfect skin, and those eyes. You have a face like an angel, Sherica."

"Yeah, right." By then we were sitting in an all-night diner, eating toasted cheese sandwiches with tomato soup.

"I'm absolutely serious! I didn't expect—I wasn't nearly as pretty when I was your age."

She was sure pretty now, even with her brown hair

yanked back in a ponytail, and no makeup, and dripping soup on herself.

"Oh, Sherica . . ." She teared up again. "Are you . . ." She hesitated. "Are you all right?"

"Yeah, Mom, or at least I think I will be once we finish up with the cops and stuff."

"You don't have to tell them anything you don't want to. Me, either."

Already I felt pretty sure I was going to want to tell her everything.

She asked, "Finished eating?"

"Yup."

"Ready to go home?"

I couldn't speak. I had to nod. We barely said a thing as a taxi took us to an airport, but we hung onto each other's hands. A private pilot was there, standing beside a little airplane waiting to take us back to Latrobe. That was how Mom had got to Nashville so fast—on Angel Flight, an organization of pilots who give rides in emergencies.

"Have you ever flown?" Mom asked me.

I shook my head.

"Are you scared?"

"No, I think it'll be nice." The airplane was white. Just as I'd expected, it sailed like an airy boat in the night sky.

Sailed. Saylor. Monica Saylor Suloff. Sherica Suloff.

"We moved a lot of places," I told Mom, "and I had a lot of different names. It feels awesome to be Sherica again."

What with the engine noise and its being so late at night, we didn't talk much. But Mom kept looking at me, like, checking to make sure I was real; and every once in a while she would touch me. My hair. My cheekbone. My hand. For a long time she held my hand between both of hers.

When we got to the Latrobe airport, there was a searchlight—the pilot called it a beacon—to guide us safely down out of the sky and home.